Billy the Conkerer

Billy the
Conkerer

Written and illustrated by
Wendy Smith

PUFFIN BOOKS

For Ted and Robert

PUFFIN BOOKS

Published by the Penguin Group
Penguin Books Ltd, 27 Wrights Lane, London W8 5TZ, England
Penguin Putnam Inc., 375 Hudson Street, New York, New York 10014, USA
Penguin Books Australia Ltd, Ringwood, Victoria, Australia
Penguin Books Canada Ltd, 10 Alcorn Avenue, Toronto, Ontario, Canada M4V 3B2
Penguin Books (NZ) Ltd, Private Bag 102902, NSMC, Auckland, New Zealand

Penguin Books Ltd, Registered Offices: Harmondsworth, Middlesex, England

First published 1999
1 3 5 7 9 10 8 6 4 2

Filmset in Bembo Schoolbook

Printed in Hong Kong by Midas Printing Ltd

British Library Cataloguing in Publication Data
A CIP catalogue record for this book is available from the British Library

ISBN 0–141–30065–5

Billy came from a big, strong family.
Dad was a bouncer at The Dungeon
Disco, Mum drove a cement lorry, and
even Billy's little sister, Madge, had the
strength of Hercules. She was a Junior
Weight-lifting Champion.

Poor Billy had spindly little arms like a stick insect and a pale, delicate face. He didn't like lifting weights and doing exercises. Billy liked peace and quiet.

"Coming down the gym, Billy?" asked his dad, popping his head round the door.

"Not tonight, Dad," said Billy. "I've got things to do." Billy liked to spend his time inventing stuff on the computer.

Billy's mum worried about him.
"He's so frail," she sighed.

"He's a wimpy weed," said his sister,
Madge, helpfully tossing bags of
cement into Mum's lorry.

3

Madge had legs and arms like logs.
She could swim a hundred lengths and
chop wood karate-style. No one ever
wanted to pick a fight with her. She
walked to school with Billy every day.
"Just in case you get picked on," said
Madge.

"I know," said Billy. "But I can look after myself."

All the same, he was glad to be with Madge when Killer Karl and his gang walked by. Killer Karl was the biggest and beefiest bully in the school.

Billy's dad also worried about him. "You spend far too much time on that computer. You need to build up your strength. Eat some stodge and do some exercises. Otherwise," Dad said, "you're going to get biffed."

"Yes, Dad," said Billy, giving in.

Billy ate beans – loads of them. He ate chips with them too. He did sit-ups and press-ups and workouts. But Billy stayed as thin as a needle.

"Sit-ups are silly and beans are boring," he announced. "I like playing with my computer."

Billy's mum and dad were more worried than ever. They went to see the Head Teacher, Miss Thompson.

"He's a lovely, sensitive boy," said Miss Thompson. "And so clever with his computer."

"Hum," said Mum.

"Ho," said Dad. "We'd like him to do extra gym."

"I'll ask Mr Bull, the P.E. teacher, to
see what we can do," replied Miss
Thompson.

Mr Bull looked at Billy's long,
thin legs and decided to give him
tree-climbing exercises.

"That way you can stay out of
trouble," said Mr Bull.

Billy became very good at
tree-climbing. At breaktime he liked to
sit in the chestnut tree by the school
gate. He could see what was going on
from up there and think of ideas for his
computer in peace.

Then, one lunchtime, Billy saw Killer Karl stroll back through the school gates. Where had he been? Billy wondered.

Karl had an even meaner look in his eye than usual and a smug grin. Indeed, he was feeling very pleased with himself that day. Not only had he sneaked out of History, but Barbarians the hairdresser's had given him the fiercest haircut in town.

Just as Karl passed underneath the tree, Billy knocked down a shower of chestnuts by accident.

CLACK, CLUMP, WALLOP!

The chestnuts stuck in Karl's new haircut.

Eek! thought Billy, I've had it now.

"Ha, ha!" he giggled nervously as Killer Karl looked up.

"Come down!" cried Karl, starting to climb the tree.

Yet more conkers came pouring
down as Billy sped to the top.

"That's a great haircut," said Billy,
trying not to laugh.

"It's war," shouted Karl. "I'll get
even with you for this."

Billy watched Karl stumble home
before anyone else could see him. To
his surprise Billy felt brave. I'm quicker
than beefy old Karl, he thought. I beat
him to the top.

At home that evening, Karl was snivelling in the bathroom. He was still picking out the chestnuts from what was left of his hair. His mum called up the stairs, "You've a friend at the door." A nice-looking boy, thought his mum, a nice, clean, polite boy.

"You look like you've had a fright," said Billy boldly. "How about a duel? With conkers?" he asked Karl.

"Yer," said Karl, who was really a weed inside. "Yer. I've never been challenged to a duel before. That's cool."

Karl was worried. Karl didn't fancy himelf in tights and a cloak. He had knobbly knees. He rang his friend, Bulldog, to make up the conkers.

"Get good hard ones, Bulldog. It won't take long to beat that wimp and then I'll show *him* a new haircut."

Meanwhile, Billy was making up a perfect conker formula on his computer. He sorted out the best size of conkers, when to shell them and how long the string should be for the best biffing action. He even worked out how many biffs it should take to win. Madge made posters:

FIGHT OF THE CENTURY.
KARL THE CONKER ZONKER
PLAYS BASHA BILL.

All week Billy worked on his conker kit.

He boiled them.

He steamed them.

He soaked conkers in polish, in lemonade, in porridge.

He tested them on his family.

News of the duel had spread round the school. And on the day of the contest, for once, the chip shop was empty and the playground was full.

Billy's conkers were as hard as steel. Billy was quick and Karl was slow. BIFF! BIFF!

After three rounds, Karl's conker began to split.

"I'm the conker zonker," said Billy as Karl's conker splattered into a hundred pieces.

"The winner," declared Madge.

Billy became popular overnight.

No one had ever dared to challenge Killer Karl before.

"What's your secret, Billy?" asked Lola, one of Billy's classmates.

"Oh," said Billy, "it's a magic formula I worked out on the computer."

"Show us your computer," said Harris.

"Can we come and look too?" said Jock and Jack.

"Sure," said Billy. "Come tomorrow afternoon. For tea."

Meanwhile, Killer Karl was feeling sore. His mum was making him grow out his new haircut. Soon he began to look quite sweet and no one wanted to be in his gang any more. He began to

take a keen interest in computers.

Billy entered the National Conker League. He grew little muscles. He grew bigger muscles. He smashed his way through to the finals and won the Conker Zonker Prize.

Billy became famous and went on TV.

"Such a lovely, sensitive boy," said Miss Thompson.

"Such a big, strong boy," said Billy's mum and dad.

"Yes," said Madge, lifting him up with one hand. "That's our Billy. Billy the Conkerer."